Babar the King
follows
Babar's Travels and
The Story of Babar

JEAN DE BRUNHOFF

BABAR
THE KING

METHUEN CHILDREN'S BOOKS

LONDON

King Babar and Queen Celeste
led a happy life
in the country of the elephants.
Peace had been signed with the rhinoceroses.
Their friend, the old lady,
had gladly agreed to stay with them.
She often told stories to the elephant children,
and her little monkey, Zephir,
sat up in a tree and listened too.

Leaving the old lady with Queen Celeste, Babar
with Cornelius, the oldest and wisest
"This place is so beautiful that every morning
We must build
Our houses will be by the water
Zephir who was with them

went for a walk along the shores of the big lake
of the elephants, and said to him:
when I wake up, I should like to see it.
our town here.
in the midst of flowers and birds."
was trying to catch a butterfly.

While chasing the butterfly
Zephir met his friend, Arthur,
the little cousin of the King and Queen,
who was enjoying himself, looking for snails.
Suddenly they saw
one, two, three, four dromedaries,
five, six, seven dromedaries,
eight, nine, ten ....
so many that they could no longer count them.
"Will you please tell us where King Babar is?"
said the leader of the dromedaries.

Arthur and Zephir
led the dromedaries to Babar.
They had brought his heavy luggage
and all the things he had bought
when on his honeymoon abroad.
Babar said, "Thank you, dromedaries.
You must be tired: rest for a while
in the shade of the palm trees."
Then, turning to the old lady
and Cornelius, he added,
"Now we shall be able
to build our town."

Having called a meeting of the elephants,
Babar stood on a box, and
in a loud voice spoke these words:
"My friends,
in these trunks and bales and cases
I have presents for all of you –
dresses, hats, silks,
paint-boxes, drums,
tins of peaches, feathers, racquets,
and many other things.
I will give them to you
as soon as we have built our new town.
This town, the town of the elephants,
I propose that we call Celesteville
in honour of your Queen."
"Hear! Hear!"
cried all the elephants,
raising their trunks in the air.

The elephants set to work at once.
Arthur and Zephir distributed the tools, and
Babar showed each one the work he had to do.
He drew plans of
the streets and houses;
he ordered one party to cut down trees,
another to carry stones,
and others again to saw wood and to dig foundations.
How eagerly they all set to work!
The old lady put on the gramophone.
Babar played the trumpet
now and again, for a change;
like all elephants
he loved music.
Thoroughly enjoying themselves,
They hammered, and pulled, and pushed,
and dug, and tossed, and carried,
flapping their great ears the while.

In the great lake
the fishes grumbled to each other.
"We can no longer sleep in peace,"
they said,
"those elephants make too much noise!
What can they be doing?
When we jump out of the water
we have no time to see anything properly.
We must ask
the frogs."

The birds, too, met together
to talk about the elephants:
the pelicans and flamingoes,
the ducks and the ibises,
and even the tiniest ones.
They twittered and chirped and sang,
and the parrots grew enthusiastic,
repeating over and over again:
"Come and see Celesteville, most beautiful of towns!
Come and see Celesteville, most beautiful of towns!"

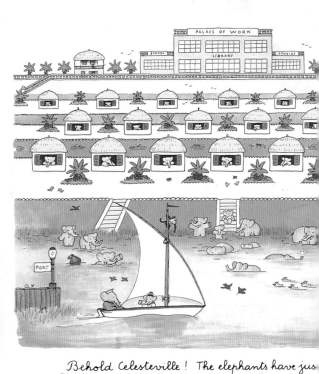

Behold Celesteville! The elephants have jus
Babar, with Arthur and Zephir, is sailing roun
Each elephant ha
The old lady's house is at the top on the lef
All the windows look ou
The Palace of Work is next to the Palac

...inished building it, and are now resting or bathing.

...t in his boat, admiring his new Capital.

...house of his own.

...nd Babar's at the top on the right.

...ver the big lake.

...f Pleasure, which is very convenient.

Babar now kept his promise:
to each elephant he gave a present,
together with good working-clothes
and lovely holiday-costumes.
When they had thanked their King
the elephants went dancing home.

Babar arranged that on the following Sunday,
after dressing up in their best,
the elephants should have a Garden Party
in the grounds of the Palace of Pleasure.
So the gardeners had plenty to do,
raking the paths, watering the flowers,
and planting out the beds.

The little elephants planned a surprise
for Babar and Celeste.
They asked Cornelius
to teach them
the song of the elephants.
It was Arthur's idea.
They practised hard
to get it perfect by Sunday!

SONG OF THE ELEPHANTS

MELODY

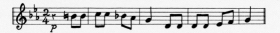

Pa-ta-li di-ra-pa-ta crom-da crom-da ri-pa-lo

Pa-ta Pa-ta Ko Ko Ko.............

WORDS

1ST VERSE

PATALI DIRAPATA
CROMDA CROMDA RIPALO
PATA PATA
KO KO KO

2ND VERSE

BOKORO DIPOULITO
RONDI RONDI PEPINO
PATA PATA
KO KO KO

3RD VERSE

ÉMANA KARASSOLI
LOUCRA LOUCRA PONPONTO
PATA PATA
KO KO KO

NOTE: This song is the old chant of the Mammoths, Cornelius himself doesn't know what the words mean —

The cooks set to work with all speed
to prepare cakes and pastries of every kind.
Queen Celeste helped them.
Zephir tasted the vanilla cream
to see if it was sweet enough.
He dipped his finger in it,
then his hand, then his arm.
Arthur longed to plunge in his trunk.

For one last taste
Zephir leaned over and put out his tongue,
and, plop! in he fell.
The head cook was very angry,
and fished Zephir out by the tail.
Poor Zephir was a dreadful sight,
yellow and slimy.
Celeste took him away to wash him.

Sunday came at last. In the garden
walked about dressed in their best. The children
The refreshments were delicious What a glorious day
And here you see the old lady

f the Palace of Pleasure the elephants
sang their song and Babar kissed them all.
The time passed only too quickly!
rranging the last game of hide and seek.

The next day
after their morning bathe in the lake,
the elephant children went to school.
They were always happy to see
their dear mistress, the old lady.
Their lessons with her were
never dull.

When she had set the little ones to work,
she taught the bigger ones. "What is
three times three?" "Eight", said Arthur.
"No, nine", said Ottilie, who sat next to him.
"Nine: a cat-o'-nine-tails", shouted Zephir.
"Nine", echoed Arthur,
"I will not forget that again."

The elephants who
were too old to go to school
each chose a profession or trade.
For example:
Tapitor was a shoemaker, Pilophage an officer,
Capoulosse a doctor, Barbacol a tailor,
Podular a sculptor,
and Hatchibombotar swept and watered the roads.
Doulamor was a musician, Olur a mechanic,
Poutifour a farmer, Fandago a scholar,
Justinien a painter and Coco a clown.
When Capoulosse had holes in his shoes
he took them to Tapitor, and
when Tapitor was ill Capoulosse attended him.
If Barbacol wanted to put a statuette
on his mantel-piece he told Podular,
and when Podular's jacket was worn out
Barbacol measured him for a new one.
Justinien painted Pilophage's portrait,
and Pilophage defended him against his enemies.
Hatchibombotar kept the streets tidy,
Olur repaired motor cars,
and, when they were tired,
Doulamor played to them.
After solving difficult problems,
Fandago ate fruit grown by Poutifour.
As for Coco,
he made them all laugh.

TAPITOR CAPOULOSSE FANDAGO BARBACOL

PODULAR PILOPHAGE JUSTINIEN DOULAMOR

POUTIFOUR HATCHIBOMBOTAR OLUR COCO

In Celesteville
the elephants work all the morning;
in the afternoon they do whatever they like.
They play, go for walks, read and dream.
Babar and Celeste loved a game of tennis
with Mr. and Mrs. Pilophage.

Cornelius, Fandago, Podular and Capoulosse
preferred to play bowls.
The little elephants and Arthur and Zephir
enjoyed themselves
with Coco, the clown.
There was also the pond for boats,
and they had many other games besides.

But what the elephants loved best of a

as the Theatre in the Palace of Pleasure.

The first thing every morning
Hatchibombotar watered the streets
with his motor watercart.
When Arthur and Zephir met him
they quickly took off their shoes,
and followed bare-foot.
"What a lovely shower-bath!"
they shouted.
One day, unfortunately,
Babar saw them:
"No dessert for you, you naughty children!"
he cried.

Like all little boys, Arthur and Zephir
were always up to mischief;
but they were not lazy.
At the old lady's house, Babar and Celeste
were astonished to hear them playing
the violin and 'cello.
"It's wonderful!" cried Celeste,
and Babar said:
"Children, I am pleased with you.
Go to the cake-shop and
choose whatever you like."

Arthur and Zephir enjoyed
eating the cakes,
but it gave them even more pleasure
to hear Cornelius read out,
on prize-giving day:
"First prize for music.
Equal, Arthur and Zephir."
They went back to their seats
feeling very proud.
After he had given away the prizes
Cornelius made a very fine speech:

" And now, a happy holiday to you all !"
he cried,
and sat down
amid loud cheers,
forgetting that his beautiful hat
lay on his chair.
He flattened it out completely.
"It's just like a pancake!"exclaimed Zephir.
Cornelius looked at it
in horror.
What was he to wear at the coming Fête?

The old lady promised Cornelius
to trim his old bowler with feathers,
and, to cheer him up, she invited him
for a ride in the beautiful roundabout
that had just been ordered by Babar.

Podular had carved the animals,
Justinien had painted them,
and the machinery had been put in by Olur.
They were all three very clever.

The King's mechanical horse
had also been made by them.
Olur greased it well, and the King mounted it
to give it a final trial
before the Grand Fête
to commemorate the anniversary
of the foundation of Celesteville.

In glorious weather the Grand Fête took place. At the hea
Cornelius, wearing his retrimmed hat, followed;
All the elephants who were not in the processio

the procession marched Arthur and Zephir and the band.
en came the soldiers, and the arts and crafts guilds.
atched the memorable pageant.

On his way home
after the Fête
Zephir saw
a strange looking stick

He stooped to pick it up.
Horror!
It was a snake
that rose with a hiss

and cruelly bit
the old lady,
who had taken Zephir
in her arms.

Arthur hit out furiously
and broke his trumpet
on the serpent's back
and killed it.

The old lady,
with a swelling arm,
hastened
to the hospital.

Dr. Capoulosse
attended her.
He at once injected
serum.

Feeling miserable,
Zephir sat
near his mistress
who was very ill.

"I cannot tell
till tomorrow
whether she will recover,"
said the doctor to Babar.

On his way from the hospital
Babar heard cries of "Fire! Fire!"
Cornelius' house was in flames.
The staircase was already ablaze;
but, after many efforts, the firemen succeeded
in rescuing Cornelius by the window.
He was half suffocated,
and injured by a falling beam.
Capoulosse was quickly called,
and gave him first aid
before removing him to hospital.
This terrible fire
was caused by a lighted match
that Cornelius had thrown
towards an ashtray;
but the match, still alight,
had fallen into the waste paper basket.

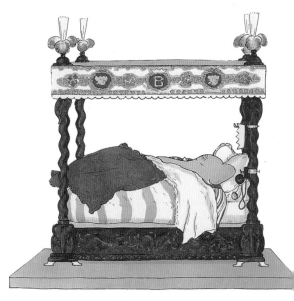

That night
when Babar went to bed,
he shut his eyes but could not sleep.
"What a dreadful day!" he thought.
"It began so well;
why did it finish so badly?
Before these two accidents
we were so happy and peaceful
in Celesteville.

"We had forgotten what unhappiness was!
Oh, my old Cornelius,
and you, my dear old lady, my friend,
I would give my crown
to see you both cured !
Capoulosse ought to telephone news of you.
How long this night seems,
and how restless I am ! "

At last Babar fell asleep.
He tossed and turned, and then dreamed.
He heard a Knocking at his door,
Tap! Tap! Tap!
Then a voice said :
"It is I, Misfortune,
with some of my companions.
We have come to visit you."
He looked out of the window
and saw a hideous old woman,
surrounded by a crowd of ugly creatures.
As he opened his mouth to shout :
"Shoo! Off with you !"
he heard a sweet sound
that made him pause,—
Frr! Frr! Frr!
like the wings of birds in flight
and he saw coming towards him ......

...... glorious elephants with wings,
who chased Misfortune
far from Celesteville,
and brought with them
Happiness —
At that moment Babar awoke
and felt better.

Babar dressed and hastened to the hospital.
Oh, Joy! What did he see?
His two dear invalids
walking in the garden.
He could hardly believe his eyes.
"I have quite recovered,"
said Cornelius,
"but all this excitement
has made me feel as hungry as a hunter.
Come and have breakfast,
and after that we will rebuild
my house."

A week later
in Babar's drawingroom
the old lady addressed her friends.
She said:
"Remember that in this life
we must never lose heart.
The wicked snake has not killed me,
and Cornelius is well again.
Let us work and play with a will
and we shall always be
happy."

Ever since that day
in the country of the elephants
they have all lived
in peace and happiness.

This edition of *Babar the King* follows the first edition in English;
it includes the hand-written lettering, which was a feature
of the early titles in the series.

First published in Great Britain 1936
by Methuen & Co Ltd
Copyright Librairie Hachette, Paris
This presentation published 1991
by Methuen Children's Books
A Division of the Octopus Publishing Group
Michelin House, 81 Fulham Road, London SW3 6RB
This presentation copyright ©
Methuen Children's Books 1991
All rights reserved

Printed and bound in Hong Kong
by Wing King Tong

ISBN 0 416 18442 1